First published 2018 by Egmont UK Limited
This edition published in Great Britain in 2020 by Dean,
an imprint of Egmont UK Limited
2 Minster Court, 10th Floor, London EC3R 7BB
www.egmont.co.uk

Text by Clement C. Moore
Illustrations by Louise Pigott

ISBN 978 0 6035 7594 5
70041/004
Printed in China

Egmont takes its responsibility to the planet and its inhabitants very seriously.
We aim to use papers from well-managed forests run by responsible suppliers.

THE NIGHT
BEFORE CHRISTMAS

Clement C. Moore
Illustrated by Louise Pigott

DEAN

'Twas the night before Christmas,
 when all through the house
  Not a creature was stirring, not even a mouse;

The stockings were hung by the chimney with care,
In hopes that Saint Nicholas soon would be there.

The children were nestled all snug in their beds,
While visions of sugar plums danced in their heads,
And Mama in her kerchief, and I in my cap,
Had just settled our brains for a long winter's nap

When out on the lawn there arose such a clatter,
I sprang from my bed to see what was the matter.
Away to the window I flew like a flash,
Tore open the shutters and threw up the sash.

The moon on the breast of the new-fallen snow,
Gave a lustre of midday to objects below;
When, what to my wondering eyes did appear,
But a miniature sleigh, and eight tiny reindeer.

With a little old driver, so lively and quick,
I knew in a moment he must be Saint Nick.
More rapid than eagles his coursers they came,
And he whistled, and shouted, and called
    them by name:

"Now, Dasher! Now, Dancer!
    Now, Prancer and Vixen!
On, Comet! On, Cupid!
    On, Donner and Blitzen!
To the top of the porch, to the top of the wall!
Now dash away, dash away, dash away all!"

As dry leaves that before the wild hurricane fly
When they meet with an obstacle,
    mount to the sky;
So up to the housetop the coursers they flew,
With the sleigh full of toys –
    and Saint Nicholas too.

And then in a twinkling, I heard on the roof
The prancing and pawing of each little hoof –
As I drew in my head, and was turning around,
Down the chimney Saint Nicholas
    came with a bound.

He was dressed all in fur, from his head to his foot,
And his clothes were all tarnished with ashes and so
A bundle of toys he had flung on his back,
And he looked like a pedlar just opening his pack.

His eyes – how they twinkled! His dimples,
    how merry!
His cheeks were like roses, his nose like a cherry!
His droll little mouth was drawn up like a bow,
And the beard on his chin was as white as the snov

The stump of a pipe he held tight in his teeth,
And the smoke it encircled his head like a wreath.
He had a broad face and a little round belly
That shook when he laughed, like a bowl full of jelly.

He was chubby and plump, a right jolly old elf,
And I laughed when I saw him, in spite of myself;
A wink of his eye and a twist of his head
Soon gave me to know I had nothing to dread;

He spoke not a word, but went straight
   to his work,
And filled all the stockings, then turned
   with a jerk,
And laying his finger aside of his nose,
And giving a nod, up the chimney he rose;

He sprang to his sleigh, to his team gave a whistle,
And away they all flew like the down of a thistle.
But I heard him exclaim, ere he drove out of sight –

"Happy Christmas
to all, and to all a good night!"